FINDING

Purpose

IN THE STORM

FINDING

Purpose

IN THE STORM

CYNTHIA B. JACKSON

[handwritten inscription:] Mary, May you continue to Walk in Purpose! :)

FINDING PURPOSE IN THE STORM

ISBN 13: 978-0-578-56358-9

DISCLAIMER

To purchase additional books:
info@cynthiabjackson.com
www.cynthiabjackson.com

Cover Design:
Anointed Press Graphics, Inc.
www.anointedpressgraphics.com
copyright (c) 2021

Layout by:
Anointed Press Publishers
(a subsidiary company of Anointed Press Graphics, Inc.)
11191 Crain Highway
Cheltenham, MD 20623
301-782-2285

WHAT OTHER'S ARE SAYING

"Cynthia B. Jackson is a woman of God and it comes through in everything she does. She is an author, and is also known as a mighty prayer warrior. She carefully handles the word of God and intentionally uses her gifts and talents to encourage others to "Live Beyond their Expectation."

-La-Kita Gilmore
Founder & CEO Women of Purpose

Cynthia B. Jackson- "CBJ" is an anointed Woman of God. God has used her to speak prophetically into my life regarding my Purpose and Legacy. She is an amazing speaker, teacher, mentor and author. She has a sincere passion to encourage and inspire others to their greatness in Christ through Speaking Encouraging Words-S.E.W., and is a powerful prayer warrior in the Kingdom of God."

-Dr. Honney Lavern Barner
Author, Entrepreneur and Philanthropist.

ACKNOWLEDGEMENT

I want to thank Jesus Christ for finding me when I was lost, calling me out into His Purpose when I tried to stay in my mess, and keeping me close when the distractions of life tried to pull me out of the protection of His almighty wings. I want to thank my wonderful husband, James Eric Jackson, Sr., for supporting me through each assignment God has given me to fulfill. Our sons, James Jr. and Jaryn Elijah thank you for giving me the title of mother, and my daughter-in-law, Kelsey Nkrumah-Jackson. Thank you, Kelsey, for being a blessed addition to our family. I thank God, He chose you to be my daughter-in-love.

I also want to thank my mother, Betty Jean Baker-Castille. I thank God for choosing you to be my mother and my sisters and brothers who encouraged me along the way. Each one of you has been a blessing to me.

TABLE OF CONTENT

PREFACE

My 9th-grade teacher's name was Ms. Hurst. Out of all of my high school teachers, I remember her the most because she was the first person to recognize my writing abilities. Even now, I can still see her stopping at my desk to hand me a paper I had written for an assignment. I recall her saying to me, "Cynthia, you are a good writer."

At that time, it went in one ear and out of the other. I cannot even recall how I responded to her compliment. I went about my life and never really thought about what she said regarding my writing. That was until I took my very first English writing course in college. I turned in a writing assignment, and the instructor said to me, "Cynthia, you are an excellent writer."

But this time, these words regarding my writing abilities got my attention. I paused and pondered on what my instructor said to me. The Holy Spirit then brought me back to the compliment that my 9th-grade teacher, Ms. Hurst, said to me, "Cynthia, you are a good writer." It was at that moment that I got a glimpse of my writing abilities.

Each time I would write, I would get better and better at it. So much so that friends, family members, and co-workers would ask me to write their letters, emails, and other correspondences. I enjoyed writing for others. But my most immense joy came when I began to write the words that God began to reveal to me. As I meditated on God's words and prayed, the melody of words flowed out of me. I would write poems, declarations, sermons, and love letters to the Lord.

As the words flowed from my heart to the paper, I could not believe it was me writing all of these words. Not only that, but the words I was writing were a blessing and encouragement to me. I knew then; it was God using me to express Himself through my writings. I would write a poem, read it the next day, and think, "surely I did not write this." Although I got a glimpse of my writing abilities in 9th-grade and early on in college, I had no idea where my writing would take me and how God would use it to bless me and others. I can boldly say with confidence that God has called me to be a writer. He has not just called me to write my words, but He has called me to write His words, and for this, I am so grateful.

"Finding Purpose in The Storm" is the manifestation of God's gift in my life. This book is my testimony of how Jesus revealed Himself to me when the storms of life were trying to take me under and take me out. God not only told me who I was, but He also showed me what I could do for Him and through Him. God showed me my purpose!

My prayer is as you read my story, you will find encouragement not to give up or give in to the storms of life that are attempting to capsize your purpose in Christ. God's divine word is over your life. He is dropping nuggets of who you are, so don't dismiss them. Even in the storms of life, take notice. He is reminding you what He has given you has to be shared with the world. As you read each chapter, I encourage you to see yourself living beyond the storm and doing what God has called you to do!

INTRODUCTION

In Mark chapter 4, Jesus said to His disciples, "Let us cross over to the other side." I can imagine the disciples may have thought this was going to be just another boat ride. However, this boat ride soon turned into a fear session among them. A great windstorm arouses, and the waves beat unto the boat so that it was already filling. (Mark 4:37) And while all of this was going on, Jesus was in the stern, sleeping on a pillow. His disciples were distraught and woke Him up and said, "Teacher, do you not care that we are perishing?" Jesus arose and rebuked the wind and said to the sea, "Peace, be still!" And the wind ceased, and there was a great calm. At this time, I don't believe the disciples knew who was in the boat with them. They called Him a teacher, but He was much more than just their teacher. He was their Messiah, the son of the living God who had the authority to calm the wind and the sea. The disciples thought they would die in the storm, but the storm was not there to kill them; it revealed who Jesus was.

Every time I read the testimony about Jesus, His disciples, and the storm, I think about the storms I've experienced in my life. Like the disciples, I had the same feeling of fear and desperation. I thought my storms were going to take me under, and I was going to die. But this was not the truth. The truth is the storms compelled me to call on the name of Jesus, and when I did, He showed me who He was; my Savior and a restorer of my soul.

He wasn't just a deity sitting in heaven looking down on me, making sure I did everything right and punishing me when I didn't. No, He is my friend, my advocate, my deliverer, and my Savior. The one who sits at the right hand of God, the Father, making intercession for you and me. And just like He heard the disciple's cry of fear in the boat, He hears our every cry. Even when the storms of life try to silence our voice and attempt to keep us out of His presence, He still hears our cry for help.

In 1999, a storm came to the shores of my heart.

I was unprepared for what would wash up once the waters were rescinded. My storm destroyed the image I had of my life. I thought I had it all safe and secured, but a tsunami exposed the breaks and gaps in my fragile foundation of life. I was broken, disappointed, fearful, and unsure of anyone and everything. Although I was experiencing tough trials and being tested in every part of my life, I know now that God had a plan for my life, even when I did not know what that plan was. The storms that occurred in my life were never meant to drown me but were there so that I could know without a shadow of a doubt that Jesus is who I needed and who I could trust.

Fear, inadequacy, and sadness are designed to steal what God has given us and what He has called us to do. For many years, I allowed all of these things to become my oracle. They told me my future and how it would look, and I believed and received every word. Fear words to me were, "you will never be accepted, no one cares about you, so why bother trying." Inadequacy's words to me were, "who do you think you are? She is prettier and smarter than you; she deserves to be where you want to be."

Sadness words to me were, "nothing good will ever happen to you, so there is no need to be happy." These statements were lies, but I did not know how to respond or challenge them. I provided them a space in my heart and mind, and they occupied these spaces very well.

However, through my storm, I was able to hear God's voice louder than any other voice. Just like thunder, His voice drowned out every voice that was intimidating me. Jesus entered my heart, grabbed the megaphone, and told the voices their lease had expired, and they were being evicted. God announced His truth to my heart, and I received it and began to follow His voice and leading. The more I was in the presence of the Lord, the more I heard His plans for my life and not the forecast of the storm. The voices of fear, inadequacy, and sadness slowly faded away in the background. God's word issued them their eviction notices, and I was no longer going to make a space for them anywhere in my life.

Receiving the revelation of who you are in Jesus is so important. When you know who you are, the storms of life will not intimidate you. You will have confidence in Jesus' ability to give you what you need so you can weather the storm and come out on the other side with a greater insight into who He is and who you are. This book is a transparent look at my life, but it is also filled with words of encouragement and hope. When you read this book, I believe it will stir your heart to believe in Jesus and go after what He has for you, even during the storms of disappointments in your life. You are alive to fulfill God's plan for your life. The storms of your life will reveal your purpose if you remain in the presence of our Lord, Jesus Christ. He is with you on the boat; call on His name and watch Him manifest His power in your life!

CHAPTER 1

"PURPOSE"

The word *"Purpose"* is defined as the reason for which something exists. We exist because God wanted us to be here on this earth to fulfill His Purpose. He wants us to acknowledge His hand in our creation and receive the truth. God is the author of our life. God gives us gifts and talents that we are to use that reveal the glory of who He is in our lives. When we are aligned with His purpose, we can manifest the reason(s) why He created us.

I struggled with knowing who I was and most definitely struggled with knowing what God called me to do. It wasn't until I was 30 years old that I got a glimpse of who I was. Before this, I was living life one day at a time, not being purposeful or intentional about anything spiritual in my life. I was active in doing things that satisfied my desires and needs, but not God's purpose. Were these things wrong? No, they were not! But I was not living out the purpose God had intended for me when He created me. Before having an encounter with the Lord. My focus was making sure everyone else around me was complete. I was a certified "people pleaser," and I am not ashamed to say it. I think most of us have held the title of "people pleaser."

One of the characteristics of a "people pleaser" is focusing on making sure everyone else is happy while forgetting about yourself in the process. I did not know who I was, so I found satisfaction in telling myself how great I was for helping others meet their goals and walk out their purpose. God wants us to find joy in what He has called us to do, which is walking out our God-given purpose. It is okay to assist others in meeting their goals to fulfill their purpose, but helping someone else should never be at the expense of you not accomplishing what God has called you to do.

I remember when God revealed to me that I was neglecting His assignments and purpose for my life and placing all of my attention on other people's assignment and their purpose. My mother was visiting me, and she noticed I spent a lot of time helping my husband with His homework. He was a drill sergeant at that time and worked odd hours, so I was helping him gather the research notes and resources to write his college paper. My mother saw how hard I was working and asked me, "Cynthia, when will you go to school and do your own homework?" I was shocked she asked me this question, but I did stop and ponder on it.

Here I was focusing on helping and researching for my husband to complete his education goals but did not even consider that maybe, just maybe, God wanted me to go to school and get my degree as well. Okay, so there was nothing wrong with helping my husband; I was happy to help him. But I was not investing the same time and effort into what God wanted for me. I was living from a narrow viewpoint of my life. God used my mother to show me that I had what it took to do what I was doing for my husband for myself. I thank my mother for asking me this question because I did eventually do my own homework, and it resulted in a Bachelor's degree in Human Resources Management.

Every one of us has assignments God wants us to complete. However, we will never achieve them if we don't believe God can help us do it and focus on doing what He has called us to do to walk in our purpose.

Your identity is aligned with your purpose, so knowing who you are in Christ is essential. There are constant images from the world that try to get us to buy into the lie that their way is the "way" and God's way is old-fashion and no longer relevant. But this is not God's truth. Their version of our identity is counterfeit and below God's standards. Being who God called you and me to be without conforming to this world can be a challenge. But we can do "All" things through Christ, including accessing our true identity and living out our purpose for God's Glory.

As women, we are especially prone to accepting false images from the media around us. But we don't have to conform to these images to be accepted or know our true identity. If we want to know who we are and what we were created to be, all we have to do is turn to God and allow His Son and the Holy Spirit to reveal His truth to us. When we go after Jesus, the unfolding happens. He begins to show us our identity and purpose and how we can use what He reveals to edify His Kingdom and our lives. Knowing who we are in Christ allows us to be free to give our gifts and talents without any concerns of being rejected. Even if we are dismissed, it will not stop us from believing in what God has called us to do and believing in whom God has created us to be. We will look for the next opportunity or door to open from God that will allow us to express His purpose for our lives and love others in the process.

From a very young age, I constantly compared myself to others around me. In my late teens and early twenties, I noticed a cycle in my life. I would befriend someone and saw that I would begin to mimic their behavior over time. Sometimes the behavior was good, and sometimes it wasn't. It was easy for me to mirror the behaviors of others. Mainly because I did not think my own identity and purpose were worth getting to know. I thought it was normal to be like everyone else, but I did eventually realize that I had an identity crisis. I did not know who Cynthia was or why I was even placed on this earth. No one ever explained to me that I had a purpose and was unique in God's sight. It was not until I had that encounter with Jesus in 1999 that I realized God created me uniquely and I had a purpose for living. Until then, I was a lonely young lady looking for acceptance in all the wrong places. I was trying to fit in with people who were not called to be in my life, and I allowed them to remain for fear of rejection. Over time these relationships hinder me in discovering who I was in Christ.

If you have ever felt like you had to downplay who you are to fit into a particular group or be a part of a "click," I want to encourage you to walk away. If you can't walk away on your own, ask God to help you. God wants you to display His purpose for your life, so take courage and walk away. What is on the other side of your decision is the "you" God created. It may not be easy, but it will be worth it. God did not make you so you could conform to the people around you. Jesus came so that you could thrive in knowing who you are and arrive at your God-given destiny.

It is our inheritance to find out who we are in Christ and what it is that He has called us to be. It's time to let go of other peoples' identities and purpose and live out your own. You are not last in God's sight; you are the first. You are not the tail, living as an afterthought; you are ahead with God. Your identity is in Jesus Christ, and He is eager to show himself strong to you. 2 Chronicles 16:9 says, ***"For the eyes of the Lord run to and fro throughout the whole earth, to show himself strong on behalf of those whose heart is loyal to Him."*** (NKJV) He is looking for you so He can show you who you are in Him. Don't make Him look any longer. Give Him your heart, and let Him reveal His purpose for your life. You are here "On-Purpose- For Purpose!"

CHAPTER 2

"THE BEGINNING"

I was born in Cajun country. A little town named Opelousas, Louisiana. I am the third of five children. My mother was a single parent, and I did not know my father very well. We grew up learning about the Lord because my mother always had a relationship with God. She grew up with praying family members, and the church was a priority for them. She would share childhood stories of how everyone would go to church all day on Sundays, come home, eat lunch and head back to the church that evening. She told us how prayer was a priority, and my great uncle would sometimes pray all night. So, prayer warriors are in my family line, and I believe I have inherited this generational blessing.

My mother loved God, and she would often

sit down and read the bible to us. We did not know what she was saying, but we listen. I am so thankful she shared what she knew about God with her children. She worked long and hard to give us what we needed- keeping a roof over our heads and food on the table. She took what she knew about God and shared it with her children. Deuteronomy 11:18-19 says, *"Therefore you shall lay up these words of mine in your heart and in your soul, and bind them as a sign on your hand, and they shall be as frontlets between your eyes. You shall teach them to your children, speaking of them when you sit in your house, when you walk by the way, when you lie down, and when you rise up."* (NKJV) My mother manifested this scripture in her children's lives. I thank God she did not remain silent but taught us what she knew about Jesus. I am the person I am today because of her willingness to share the testimonies of God in her life with us.

We were always Baptist we went to a Baptist church. But something changed when we began going to a Pentecostal church. The name of the church was Cathedral of Faith, Church of God in Christ. The gifts of the spirit were flowing like a roaring river. I remember seeing people fall out, speak in tongues and run around the church. It was exciting to see people express themselves this way in church, but it was also a little scary as a young girl. One thing for sure, my mother's life was changing due to what was happening in that church, and it was also affecting her children's life as well.

My mother's life changed so much that she separated herself from friends and family members who were doing drugs and drinking alcohol. Family members would call us "Holy Rollers." I was not too fond of that name back then, but today I would be honored to wear that title of a "Holy Roller". As we continued to attend church, I began to feel this tug on my heart for Jesus. However, like any other teenager, I didn't particularly appreciate going to church all the time. It seems like we were in church every day of the week and all day on Sunday. To avoid going to church, my sister and I would leave the house and go to a friend's house or the local park, hoping my mom would leave us alone. But this plan did not work. On one occasion, we went to the park to avoid going to church. We thought we were too far away to get back home in time to go to church, which is what we wanted. But my mother was so wise; she knew our motive and politely called a taxi cab to pick us up and deliver us to the church. We were hanging out with our friends, and all of a sudden, we hear the taxi cab driver call our names (it's a small town, so everyone knows everyone) and tells us my mom instructed him to pick us up and drop us off at church. We were embarrassed, and of course, our friends did not let us forget this moment. After this, she made sure we stayed close to home on bible study nights and Sunday services.

Although I did not like going to church, her requirement for me to be in the church was a true blessing. As I look back, going to church gave me the foundation I needed to pursue God. I had a reference point of who God was, I knew Jesus was real, and I could call on Him, even if it were only when I was in need or trouble. I thank God she sent a taxi cab to pick us up, made us rise early for church services, made us attend mid-week bible study and all-night shut-ins. She did not allow us to do what we wanted; she instructed and steered us to the Lord because she knew how much we would need Him in our lives. Being in a Pentecostal church helped my mother in raising her children as a single parent. All of our lives were changing, and it was for the good.

Our life at Cathedral of Faith, Church of God in Christ, was new, and I felt something pulling on my heart that I had never felt before. Although I was a young teen, there was this "pull" that I was trying to figure out. I would feel the pull when the pastor would ask, "Who would like to give their life to Christ" but I would not budge; I could not move from my seat. I was not only hearing about accepting Jesus in church, but I would hear it at school also. I know you may be thinking, "Cynthia, are you sure you heard the call to Jesus at school." And my response is, "yes, I did"! My science teacher, Mr. Green, was a Christian, and I remember he would talk to us about Jesus in class.

I know you may be thinking, if this were to occur today, Mr. Green would be unemployed, and you are probably right. I'm not sure what happened, but apparently, in the 1980's it was acceptable to talk about Jesus in public schools. Every time Mr. Green would ask us if we knew

Jesus, I felt this same "pull" on my heart, but I did not respond. Let me explain this "pull." It was like something inside me was telling me that I needed to get to know Jesus more, but each time I ignored this voice and did not act on what it was calling me to do.

The pulling on my heart finally stopped, and I will never forget the moment it did. There was an Apostolic church located on the street where we lived. This church was different from our Pentecostal church. The members wore long skirts, no makeup, all the men wore long-sleeve white shirts, and it seemed like they all lived next to each other on our street.

But they were friendly and always were together in groups. On my way home from school or just walking in the neighborhood with friends, members of this Apostolic church would stop and talk to us about Jesus. Sometimes I would listen, and other times I would try my best not to make eye contact and walk as fast as possible so they would not stop me. I know it wasn't a nice thing to do, but I was a teenager and did not want to spend my afternoon talking about Jesus. But something happened one particular night.

My sister and her then-boyfriend encountered a man who was a member of the Apostolic church. This man ministered to my sister and her boyfriend. I'm not sure what he said to them, but when they arrived back at our house, they both were crying so much that I thought someone had harmed them. The two of them could barely get words out of their mouth. My sister began to speak in the language known as tongues, just like members of our church spoke, and she was saying the name Jesus repeatedly.

I was confused and scared at the same time. My mother was not home, so no adult was present to help us process what was happening. Again, I'm not sure what the man told them, but whatever it was caused them to cry and call out the name of Jesus. As all of this was going on, I began to cry, I think in the beginning, I was crying because I was scared, but when my sister began to say the name Jesus, over and over again, I began to repeat it. As I repeated the name of Jesus, my heart began to open up like a dam, and the tears of fear became tears of surrender.

There is a song by Kirk Franklin called "Something About the Name Jesus" one of the choruses says, "The power that I feel When I call your name; It's just like fire shut up in my bones; The Holy Ghost is moving. The Holy Ghost was moving, and I finally allowed the pulling on my heart to take me right into the arms of Jesus. On that night, I gave my life to the Lord. I surrendered to the pull that had been on my heart and answered the call to salvation.

My heart was lighter, and I felt like a new person. The next day I was excited to go to school. I wanted to tell Mr. Green, my science teacher, that I had given my life to the Lord. I told him, and he was excited for me. At that time, I did not know what all of this meant, but what I did know was I felt different. It was like my heart was more attentive to God. My encounter with Jesus was seared in my heart, which changed how I saw things in my life. Following this encounter, my mom continued to take us to church, and as I sat in the church, I realized I was getting a better understanding of who Jesus was and why He came to save us from our sins. From this point on began a long journey of discovering who Jesus was and why He desired that I know more of Him.

CHAPTER 3

"STUMBLING ALONG THE WAY"

I would love to tell you from that point on I was sold out for Jesus. But this was not the case. Although I surrendered my life to Jesus, there were things in my life I still had to overcome. These things were fear, inadequacy, and sadness. I believe, when God opens our eyes to show us who He is, He also reveals who we are and show us the issues in our life that need to be eradicated.

Issues we ignored or were unaware of, but they had a considerable presence in our lives. I thought fear, inadequacy, and sadness were just who I was. I allowed these feelings to capture my affection and attention, and because of it, they found a home in my heart. I've learned over the years; whatever you give affection and attention to, you permit it to remain in your life. We need to align our affections and attention to the things of God and what He says about us. When we do this, then we live in His Will and not the enemy's lies.

I continued to attend my church, and as I stated, the church flowed powerfully in the gifts of the spirit. Services were electrifying and exciting, and you could feel the Holy Spirit moving. Our pastor could preach the paint off the walls, which was great, but there was little teaching on how to live a purpose-filled life or study the bible. His method of teaching was not wrong because we were blessed.

It was the 1980's, and this is how the church was. In my opinion, it was about the experience in church, and little thought or focus was given on how to apply the word of God in everyday living. I struggled to overcome fear, inadequacy, and sadness. For years, I fought and lost battles with these three things. I had no identity, and I continued to listen to these voices. Sadly, my inability to shut them down reinforced my lack of identity and purpose.

So, for the next several years, I stumbled along the way in my faith. Trying to live according to the bible but often failing because I had no depth of knowing who Jesus was. I call this living out "the cycle of salvation." I will talk more about the "cycle of salvation" in chapter 5. But the "cycle of salvation" means you give your life to Jesus only to find yourself back in a sinful lifestyle you swore you would never practice again. You go to church, and because God has a call upon your life, He draws you back to the altar, and you find yourself rededicating your life back to Him. Jeremiah 3:14 says, **"Return, O backsliding children," says the Lord, "for I am married to you. I will take you, one from a city and two from a family, and I will bring you to Zion**. (NKJV)

God is married to us. It does not matter how many times you have gone through "the cycle of salvation." He is not mad at you. God knew you would need Him, and each time He draws you back to the place of redemption. He was married to me, and although I felt guilty each time I went back to the altar, I am happy that He drew me back into His presence to receive His love and forgiveness. I am stumbling along the way, and I was approaching my eighteenth birthday. I was getting ready to graduate high school, and I remember my mother saying these words to me, "Once you turn eighteen, you will have to find you a job because I will no longer be receiving financial support for you." Okay, there's that fear rising again, saying, "I told you so." "What are you going to do now?" I was so afraid because I had no clue what my purpose was or what I would do. I had no aspirations of what I wanted to become. I was so fearful. I recall listening to fellow high school graduates saying they would go to college and get a degree in a specific career field. At least they had an idea. I didn't have a clue of what I wanted to do or even what I was capable of doing. I did not want to stay in Louisiana, so, I signed up for the United States Army. I thought, "I could do this! I'll join the Army and move away from home. Perfect!" I signed up for the Army in May of 1990 and was scheduled to leave in the Fall.

I went through the medical process and discovered I was not eligible because I had a heart mummer. Now I'm thinking, I cannot even get into the military. When my recruiter found out, he was not very happy. I remember him saying to me, "I am going to send you back, and the next time you tell them you are okay." So being young and not having any idea of what I wanted to do with my life, I went back through the medical process and did exactly what my recruiter instructed me to do, and I passed the exam.

My date to leave for basic training was October 1990. I remember the entire summer thinking, "do I really want to join the army?" I'm not sure where these thoughts were coming from because I had no other plans outside of joining the Army. The idea of not wanting to go to basic training would come and go, and I never shared it with anyone. One day I was in the kitchen with my mother, and she asked me, "Do you not want to join the Army"? She is very prophetic, and I believe that she sensed that I was struggling with the decision I had made. I said to her, "No, I don't want to go." She said, "tell them that you don't want to go." Her response surprised me because I remember her saying I needed to do something. After all, she would no longer be receiving financial support for me.

But it also encouraged me because it gave me a sense of relief that she would not just throw me out of the house. Not that she would have, but I viewed everything from my filter of fear, so my expectations were meager, and I did not think anything good would happen to me. So, based on my mother's advice, I go to my recruiter and tell him that I did not want to go, and to my surprise, his words were, "You have to go." I, being naïve and fearful, did not challenge his words. All the excitement of finally sharing my thoughts of not wanting to join the Army ended at that moment. I felt like someone had just put the fire out in my hot air balloon just as I was ascending high into the sky, getting ready to enjoy the new view of no military in my future. I go to basic training, and again I was terrified. I did not know what to expect and was not interested in being there at all. The arrival is as you would see in a TV movie.

The drill sergeants are yelling, and all the recruits were scrambling to find their place. We were all looking like a deer in headlights. I was exhausted because we arrived early in the morning, and with all the excitement, I had only slept for an hour the night before. As the sun rose out of the horizon, we were facing the drill sergeants once again. I thought to myself, "what have I done, and why did I not just walk away when I had the chance."

As I look back on it, it wasn't that bad. I love our military and was a military wife for over 15 years, so I understand why basic training is conducted in this manner. The military is training individuals to be soldiers and accountable to defend and support the United States Constitution and not their own way. My husband served as a drill sergeant for two years and shared many stories of how young men and women would enter basic training one way and upon graduation, would be transformed into a soldier.

It is the responsibility of a drill sergeant to take individuals and conform them from a civilian mindset to the mindset of a soldier. As Christians, this is what Jesus requires of us as well. Matthew 16:24-25 says, *"if anyone wishes to come after Me, he must deny himself, and take up his cross and follow Me. For whoever wishes to save his life will lose it, but whoever loses his life for My sake will find it."* (NKJV) We have to be all in with Jesus. There is no middle ground with serving Him. And as much as I would have liked to stay home with my family and go to basic training when I felt like it, it was not an option and never going to happen. The military did not make any provision for me to do it my way, and God does not make any provision for us to serve Him in the way we would like to serve Him or when it is convenient for us to do so. It is His way, not our way. His way leads us to life, and our method leads to roadblocks that hinder His Will from being done in our lives.

Basic training was not where I wanted to be. I was

not happy and just wanted to go home. But my time spent in basic training was not wasted. God used this time in the military to reveal a more intimate side of who He was. Even though I had backslidden, in His goodness, He still pursued me. Jeremiah 31:3, says *"the Lord hath appeared of old unto me, saying, Yea, I have loved thee with an everlasting love: therefore, with lovingkindness have I drawn thee."* (NKJV) He was drawing me even when I did not realize it. He was intentional in every aspect of my time in basic training. I thought I had missed the mark, but God was up to something; He revealed another layer of who I was in Him.

God used my time in basic training as the training ground for my prayer life. Until then, I only prayed quick prayers such as, "God help Me" or "I need you to do this, Lord." But this all changed when I began to pray to God and ask Him to get me out of basic training. I did not want to be there, so I prayed all the time. I recall getting into my wall locker and praying until I had to leave. I don't even remember what I said, but I prayed for a very long time. Listen, when you are desperate for God to move on your behalf, you have no boundaries for what you will do. My secret place of prayer was my wall locker, and I had no shame crawling into that locker and praying.

I want to encourage the person who is reading this book. You may have made a decision out of fear, but God has a way of taking that decision and turning it around for your good. Romans 8:28 says, *"And we know that ALL things work together for good to those who love God, to those who are called according to His purpose.* (NKJV) YOU ARE CALLED ACCORDING TO HIS PURPOSE! He has a plan for your life. I thought I made a huge mistake by joining the Army, and I was upset that my recruiter encouraged me to lie about my health, but God had a purpose for me being in basic training.

I started going to church in basic training, and during service, I would feel that "pull" of His presence upon my heart again. I would cry in church, go back to the barracks, get into my wall locker, and pray. One night, I remember saying in prayer, "God, if you get me out of this, I will serve you for life." Well, He answered my prayer; I went home in December 1990.

Looking back at this time in my life, my wanting to leave had more to do with me feeling inadequate and not having confidence in who I was or even what I could accomplish. I felt a lack of purpose and being there just brought out all the feelings that come with not knowing who you are, which for me was fear, inadequacy, and sadness. Although I still did not know what was in store for my life when I left the military, God answered my prayer, and I was so excited and happy to be going home.

CHAPTER 4
"THE RETURN"

When I returned home, I was happy to be home but back to square one. I had no idea of what I wanted to do with my life. I was 19 years old and remember saying, "God, thank you for getting me out of basic training, but now what?" I knew God a little bit more than before my stint in basic training but still lacked direction. I was standing in the valley of decision without any options. So, I went with the next opportunity presented to me, which was to move with my sister, who had just moved to Colorado Springs, CO. I was excited to be leaving Louisiana again, packed my bags, and got on a greyhound bus headed to a state far away from Louisiana.

When I look back at this time, I often think I would have been petrified if my nineteen-year-old daughter insisted on taking a Greyhound bus to a city thousands of miles away. But it was a different time, and I believe God protected me during my trips back and forward from Louisiana to Colorado. I arrived in Colorado Springs, CO, and was amazed at what I saw. I had lived in the South my entire life and had never seen mountains, so the view of the huge mountains took my breath away. They were beautiful and intimidating at the same time. They looked as if they would come alive and swallow up the city. I was thrilled to see my sister, and she welcomed me with open arms.

She helped me get a job at a telemarketing firm, and although it was not the ideal job, it paid our bills. I still had no clue what I wanted to do, so I returned to the flow of living, not even considering God in my plans. If you are in a similar situation, I encourage you to ask Jesus to order your footsteps. Ask Him where you need to be. Don't try to work things out according to your plans or knowledge. God will show you exactly where you need to go. He wants us to have His plans for our life hot off the presses of Heaven, and He will not be upset that you are asking Him for direction.

Although I had an incredible experience with God in basic training and learned how to pray and seek Him, I found myself conforming to my new environment. I did not pursue a church home and began to go out to clubs and participate in activities that were not acceptable to God and did not align with His Word. Initially, it was fun and exciting, but not soon after, I began to think about Jesus and everything He had done for me and how I now was ignoring my entire encounter with Him in basic training. I kept thinking, "Cynthia, what are you doing?" But Jesus, out of His love, was still drawing me. I felt the conviction in my heart each time I did things that were not of Him. He would remind me of my experience with Him, but I would brush it off and go about my sinful living.

But His love was relentless in pursuing me. Listen, we cannot get away from the love of God. There is this worship song by Cory Asbury name "Reckless Love." My favorite choruses say, "there's no shadow You won't light up, Mountain You won't climb up, coming after me. There's no wall You won't kick down, Lie You won't tear down, Coming after me."

Jesus loved me so much that although I had turned my back on Him, He was still in pursuit of me. Although I had broken my promise to serve Him for life, He did not break His promise never to leave me nor forsake me. It was the love of God drawing me back to Him. You may have done things in your life that you are not proud of and made you feel distanced from God. But I come to encourage you and let you know that God has not left you. The nudges you are feeling in your heart are reminders that God still has a purpose for your life.

Eventually, living in sin was no longer enjoyable for me. In Hebrews 11:25, it says, the pleasures of sin are for a season (paraphrased). There are pleasures with sin, but it is only for a season, and it will always cost us something. Sin pulls us away from intimacy with God and knowing His plans for our life. I was being pulled away by evil, but the Holy Spirit would often gently remind me that this was not His plan for my life. I was a "babe" in Christ, so I should have sought a church home to help me mature in my walk with the Lord.

When I moved to Colorado, I walked right into the "flow" of the sinful things around me. I subjected myself to the plans of the enemy rather than the plans of Jesus. All of a sudden, I began to yearn for His presence again, and He started to give me dreams and visions. I don't recall ever being a dreamer or, for that matter, seeing visions, but

God began to speak to me through my dreams and visions. One night, I saw a vision, and it was so profound that I will never forget it. Even as I am writing this book, I can still see the details of this vision.

I remember going to bed one night, and suddenly, I saw these three angels flying circling the moon. The sky was so clear that I could see the stars, and it was beautiful. For some reason, I sensed they were coming to get me and yelled, "I am not ready yet!" I said it so loud that I woke myself out of the vision. I had no clue how to interpret what I had just experienced and was shocked at what I had just seen. But somehow, I immediately knew God was calling me back to Him.

Even though I was not ready for Him, He was prepared for my return. After this vision, I started making decisions that were not popular with the people around me. I stopped going to the clubs and partying. I no longer wanted to live outside of God's presence. I thought about my experience in basic training and the vision I had just seen and was comforted in knowing God still had me on His mind. He wanted what was best for me even when I was settling for less. As we live out our journey with the Lord, we should never forget that His desire is for us to live a life with Him so we can know and experience His faithfulness, love, and mercy. Return to Him because He knows what's best for you. My mind and heart were shifting back to Jesus, and I embraced it.

CHAPTER 5
"THE SALVATION CYCLE"

Have you ever looked back over your life and wonder, "how did I get here?" I often think about where I would have been if I stayed in the military or never left Louisiana. I had lived in Colorado Springs, CO, for about two years, and I was ready to move back home. The Holy Spirit had revealed that this was not the life He wanted me to live, and I agreed.

I remember telling my sister I had decided to move back home to Louisiana, and she was despondent and made it clear that she did not want me to leave. We are very close and experienced many heartaches, abuse, and emotional pain growing up together, and we supported each other a lot. But I had made up my mind, and I was all set to leave. But my plans were interrupted. Okay, so let me go back a little bit and explain what interrupted my plans. About nine months before I decided to leave, I met this young man. I remember when I saw him for the first time, I said out loud, "He's going to be my husband." The words just flowed out of my mouth, and I was surprised by what I said. I was so surprised because I did not know who he was. I did not know his name, his favorite color, or anything about him. I would see him at the park or in the mall, but I did not approach him to ask him his name.

One day, my sister and I were in the mall with our guy friend, Lamont, who was like our little brother. I asked him to go and ask this young man his name. He did, and we officially met each other that day. We went on a few dates and eventually started dating. However, we did not date very long. We were on different pages at the time. I wanted a relationship with him, but he only wanted to be friends. We were both very young, trying to find our way in the world, so we ended our relationship.

I had not seen or heard from this young man for a few months, but I eventually found out from our friend Lamont that he was no longer in the Army and had moved back to Washington D.C. However, a few months later, Lamont informed me that he had moved back to Colorado Springs. I know you might be saying, "Lamont was telling you all of this young man's movements." And the answer is, yes, he was. Lamont was like my little brother, so he would tell me when he would see him or hang out with him (they had become friends).

I was no longer going out to clubs, but my sister was still going out. I would stay home, watch movies, and wait for her to come home and tell me who she saw out in the clubs. One night she returned from the club and told me she had seen this young man, and he had asked about me and wanted to see me. I was excited, but not too much because I was preparing to move home to Louisiana. So, I agreed to meet him in the local park. We talked and went on several dates after this meeting. We even went to church together and became closer. I was working at a telemarketing company, and he would meet me for lunch on occasion. It was nice to get to know him better, and I found out more about him. We went on many dates and talked about life, and it was very different from when we first met. We met a married couple who were Christians, and they would invite us over for dinner. We would talk about God and marriage, and I could feel that we were on the verge of moving into the next phase of our relationship.

One night we were at their house, and as we were leaving, I remember telling him I loved him. As I drove home, I thought about what I said when I first saw him, which was, "He is going to be my husband." Was it going to happen? Did I prophesy these words to myself, and they were getting ready to come to pass? We were moving in the direction of marriage. But how am I going to marry him, and I am moving back to Louisiana. I asked myself, "how was this relationship going to work?"

I'm moving back to Louisiana, and he is from Washington D.C. Are we going to live here in Colorado or Washington, D.C.? All of these questions were going on in my mind. Earlier in our relationship he had jokingly asked me to marry him, but now it looked like it would happen. We discussed marriage and decided that we wanted to be together, so we set a date to get married in the Fall of 1993. However, we had to change the date because we found out we were having a baby. Don't judge me; yes, we were intimate while dating; the Lord was still processing me. I am not proud of not waiting to have sex before marriage and would not recommend it to anyone for many spiritual and emotional reasons. I don't have time to write about these reasons in detail in this book. But what I will say is, it is better to get to know the person spiritually and emotionally before you connect with them intimately. We got married in the Fall of 1992 and had a beautiful baby boy in May of 1993.

To this day, my sister often asks me, "how did you know that he would be your husband," and each time I tell her, "I did not know anything; the words just flowed out of my mouth." I was even surprised by my words. At the time, I did not know much about the prophetic gift, but when I think about the words I said when I first saw him, this was indeed a prophetic word. I am so blessed to say that we've been married for 29 years, and thank God each day for him being my husband.

Although I was married, I lacked a personal vision for my life. I had a beautiful, healthy baby boy, and my focus was on my husband and our son. Again, I found myself not reading the bible and being passive in my relationship with the Lord. For almost two years, I did not go to church. At the time, I felt like it would be okay to know God but not serve Him. As I headed into my mid-twenties, I had settled in my heart serving God was too hard.

The "cycle of salvation" had become burdensome to me. One year I am good, and I am saved; the following year, I feel like I am so far away from Jesus, only to start the process all over again. Being in the "cycle of salvation" was very frustrating. For a moment during this season, I began to believe the lie that I could have more fun in the world. I thought, "look at them; they are not serving God, and they are happy and not worrying about going to hell, so it must be okay." Even now, when I think about these thoughts, it makes me upset that I would believe this lie.

I am amazed how I allowed Satan that much access into my life and allowed him to speak a lie of this magnitude and that I would even have considered it. He had this much access to my thought life because I was passive and not intentional about seeking Jesus. I allowed Satan space and opportunity in my life to sow the seeds of lies about my salvation. Satan will fill our mind with lies and deceit when we don't fill it with the truth of God's word. Reading and meditating on God's word is so important. When we give our life to Jesus but fail to learn of

Him through the word of God, we don't mature in the things of the spirit, and we believe the lies Satan speaks to us, which is designed to steal, kill and destroy our Purpose in Christ.

I believe many of us live outside of God's will for our lives and pursue the things of the world systems because we find it too hard to serve God. You may not know the source of this voice telling you to give up on serving God because it is too hard, but I want to tell you that this is not your voice. It is Satan's voice feeding these lies to you. Please don't believe this lie. Yes, we will still experience trials in this life even when we do serve God, but He is with us and will help us through every difficulty we face. It only becomes hard when we try to serve God in our strength. But, *"All things are possible with God."* (Matthew 19:26)

I was not living in God's Grace. I thought I had to do everything perfectly, and God would be mad at me if I made a mistake or sinned. Sin does separate us from God. But when we genuinely repent and turn away from our sins and surrender to Him, He embraces us and forgets we ever sinned. Jesus Christ is our advocate and our support (Psalm 18), and He is sitting at the right hand of God making intercession for you and me. When we repent of our sins, He will forgive us, draw us into intimacy with Him and teach us how to be obedient to His Word and the leading of the Holy Spirit.

I did not realize it at the time, but my mind was under attack by Satan's lies; he was after my purpose. Satan bombarded my mind with the lies, and because I accepted and believed them, he added more of his lies for me to believe. Satan's lies flooded my mind, and they reinforced my lack of identity and purpose. My life was an open book of blank pages for Satan, and he was composing his lies in my book. If I heard a voice say, "you will never be smart enough to get this job," I accepted it, and Satan recorded it in his book of lies he had created for me.

All of these words were lies coming from the pits of hell, right out of the mouth of Satan. John 8:44 says, "You are of your father the devil, and the desires of your father you want to do. He was a murderer from the beginning and does not stand in the truth, because there is no truth in him. When he speaks a lie, he speaks from his own resources, for he is a liar and the father of it. Satan is a liar whose main agenda is to steal, kill, and destroy our purpose.

He cannot stand in the truth, because there is no truth in him. When he opens up his mouth and speaks, He is lying. His resources are lies, and he is the father of lies. Again, reading and knowing the Word of God is essential. When we know the word of God, we can declare it against the lies of the enemy. Don't live out the book of lies Satan is creating for you! God wants to reveal to you His plans for your life; the plans He wrote before you were in your mother's womb. (Jeremiah 1:5) God has a master plan for our lives and wants us to not only know what it is but to live it out in the earth for His Glory.

Although I had given up on having a meaningful relationship with Jesus because I felt it was too hard to serve Him, He did not give up on me. He was still drawing me into a deeper relationship with Him. One summer day in 1998, I went about my day at home, cleaning and rearranging furniture. I turned on the TV and landed on a channel where this woman was talking about Jesus. We had just moved from Fort Benning, GA, to Fort Leonard, MO, and to be honest; I had never watched preachers on TV. The lady on TV was Joyce Meyer. Of course, I know who she is now, but I had no clue who she was at that time. As I cleaned my house and heard her voice, I started to think about Jesus. Although I had settled in my mind that it was too hard to serve Him, I listened to her words. At the end of her show, she asked if anyone wanted to rededicate their life back to Jesus. At that moment, I felt like she was talking directly to me.

As she spoke about Jesus, I began to go down memory lane. I thought about my time in school when I had initially given my life to the Lord and how excited I was. I thought about my time in basic training and remembered how God loved me through that entire process and answered my prayers. I thought about my vision of the angels in Colorado when I yelled out, "I'm not ready yet," and how my own voice woke me up from the vision. All of a sudden, with tears flowing down my face, I fell to my knees and surrendered to Jesus. I repented and asked Him to save me and forgive me for my sins. I have to be honest; this moment was a little bit different than all the other times. There was peace in the room, and I got off of my knees and continued cleaning. I remembered thinking; I need to go to church.

One of my husband's friends' wives had repeatedly been asking me to go to church with her, and I would always respond with, "No, thank you." But after my prayer with Joyce Meyer, I just knew I needed to be in church. So, I called her and asked her could I go to church with her. Every Sunday, I would attend church; God would show me that I was not destined to perish in hell. He showed me how my family and I were destined to live for Him. The words "You are destined to live" was the first word of knowledge I received from the Holy Spirit regarding my life. I now had a God vision for my life, and it was to surrender to Jesus and live for Him.

If you feel defeated and destined to fail because you have experienced the "cycle of salvation" so many times, I want to encourage you to keep believing in God's ability to love you into His perfect Will. He has a plan for your life. You are destined to live according to God's Purpose and not the enemy's plans. You don't have to settle in your sins. It is NOT too hard to serve God. Yes, you will still experience life bumps and trials, but the good news is, Jesus will be with you giving you everything you need to get through whatever comes your way. Each time I gave my life to Jesus and then gradually forgot about Him and fell back into sin, I thought I was doomed. I felt He was tired of my indecisiveness, but He was not. Jeremiah 29:11 says, *"for I know the thoughts that I think toward you, says the Lord, thoughts of peace and not of evil, to give you a future and a hope."* (NKJV) He gave me hope, and I know now that I have a future in Him. If you surrender to Him and give Him full reign in your life, He will lead you day-by-day and step-by-step into all He has for you. Take a step of faith and reconnect to Jesus Christ. You may be afraid to surrender, but it is okay, do it anyway. God will give you the courage to do it because He is calling you. Jesus is calling you to Him so that He can provide you with vision and purpose for your life.

Today is the day of your surrender. I am living proof that the "cycle of salvation" can be broken, and maintaining our connection and intimacy with our Redeemer, Jesus Christ, is possible! Romans 8:28 says, *"He causes ALL things to work together for the good of those who love Him and are called according to His purpose."* (NKJV)

Don't focus on how many times you failed to commit to following Jesus fully. Focus on how many times you heard His voice and got on your knees and asked Him into your life. Each time you reacted to His voice was a blessing, and you should praise Him for being able to hear His voice when He called you back to Him. His love and compassion for us are relentless and will draw us back to Him. You don't have to continue on the "cycle of salvation." Surrender to Jesus today and ask Him into your life. I encourage you to say this prayer below. Believe in what you are getting ready to say because it is the truth of Jesus, and it is the way to everlasting life.

> I confess with my mouth that Jesus is Lord, the Son of the only true living God-Jehovah. I believe in my heart that He was born to a virgin, died on the cross, was raised from the dead, and is sitting at the Father's right hand making intercession for humanity.

> Father in the Name of Jesus, I come before you with my heart. I ask that you come into my heart and heal me of past mistakes, hurts, and disappointments. I cannot do this independent of your presence in my life. I look to you, my redeemer, to make a way that I cannot make for myself. I repent of my sins and turn my heart away from them so that I can experience your love and you can reveal your purpose for my life. Please give

me the self-discipline and courage to turn away from things and people that would attempt to draw me back into my old ways. In Jesus' name, I pray!

CHAPTER 6

"STORMS REVEAL PURPOSE"

On a spring day in 1999, I decided to go to noon-day prayer during my lunch break. I expected to pray and head back to work and finish my workday. However, this was not what occurred. There were about five of us in prayer, and as we began to pray, one of the elders of the church looked at me and said, "you are concerned about two things, your husband salvation and being filled with the Holy Spirit with the evidence of speaking in tongues." Although I had attended a Pentecostal church as a young girl and witness other people speaking in tongues, I had never experienced it personally. However, I had been asking God to fill me with His spirit and give me the gift of speaking in tongues. I had also been praying for my husband's salvation. So, his prophetic word to me was "spot on." The elder began to pray for me, and all of a sudden, words that I could not comprehend began to flow out of my mouth, and I could not stop saying them. These words were affecting everything in me. I was six months pregnant with my second son, and I began to bend down like I was getting ready to go into labor, but I wasn't at least not in the natural. I felt like my tongues were releasing something into my life, but I did not know what it was. It felt like I was crossing over a river, and my words were moving the waters allowing me to get to the other side. I will never forget this noon-day prayer session. After prayer, I returned to work, but I could not stop speaking in tongues. That entire afternoon, I was in awe of what happened, and I was so happy God had answered my prayer of being filled with the spirit with the evidence of speaking in tongues.

I knew something had shifted in my life and opened me up to another realm of the Lord's power and authority. It felt like scales had fallen from my eyes, and I could see clearer. As the days went on, I began to see the word of God differently. When I read my bible, I could feel the words speak to me. Before speaking in tongues, I struggled to read the bible; I would get frustrated trying to enunciate names or fall asleep. Now, I could understand the testimonies in the Old Testament and some of the parables in the New Testament and be wide awake. I also had a new hunger and thirst for reading God's word and getting to know God the Father and His Son, Jesus, on a deeper level. What also happened during this time was what I like to call "the great exposure." I saw Jesus in a new way, but Jesus also exposed other things in and around me. I had crossed over to the other side, but a storm was brewing and was coming to test the very fiber of my purpose and identity. It seemed like the more I sought the Lord, the more the winds blew, and the rain poured.

I was pregnant, working, and taking care of my older son, who was five years old at the time, and I was exhausted. My husband was a drill sergeant in the Army and worked long and odd hours, so it was on me to take care of many things he usually would have taken care of. I had met this woman. She was a few years older than me, but we became good friends. Her son and my son were the same age and would play together, so they were close to our family. As time went on, we would hang out together. I would invite her and her husband over, but her husband would never be available for some reason, and she would only attend. Initially, I did not think anything of it. I just thought her husband must have been busy. Suddenly, it seems as if she wanted to hang out with my husband more than she wanted to hang out with me. For instance, she would always direct her conversations and jokes towards my husband and only look for his response. She wanted to know where my husband was and what he was doing. Although I thought it was peculiar, I did not think anything of it. Again, I was pregnant, so my focus was on getting ready to give birth to our second child and caring for our older son.

What shifted my interpretation of what was occurring was when my mother arrived to help me with my new baby. She flew in from Louisiana, and I was so happy to see her. I introduced her to this woman, and initially, she was delighted to know that I had a good friend to help me with my oldest son. But my mother began to notice the things I had seen but disregarded. She asked me why this woman was always in our home and why she only focused on my husband and his whereabouts? Okay, let me say this about my mother. She is very prophetic, and God has blessed her with the gift of discernment. My mother has always had a keen insight to decern different things in the atmosphere around her. So, when she started asking me simple questions, like, "where is her husband?" Why is she always over at your home? Initially, I would respond and say, "mama, I don't know," in a sarcastic way. But then the Lord began to open up my eyes to things I had ignored. Things I mentioned previously- always directing her conversations towards my husband and not me; looking for my husband to respond to her jokes; wanting to know where my husband would be or what he was doing. I had a blind spot on what was going on around me. I felt God was not only revealing His word to me, but He was exposing things around me as well.

These thoughts are going through my mind, and I am getting ready to have a baby. I asked the Lord, "what is going on? I just got filled with the Holy Spirit, I felt like I'm getting to know you better, but now I'm dealing with this." The very thought of infidelity regarding my husband was tearing me up on the inside. I could not think straight, and I was constantly replaying moments and times when the affair could have occurred and thought how could I have missed the signs. I was such a mess during this time. The winds of the storm I was facing began to blow fiercely around me, and my thoughts were getting the best of me.

I went into labor and gave birth to a beautiful, healthy baby boy, but my mind was so far from this joyous occasion. All the puzzle pieces of infidelity were coming together in my mind, causing me a lot of anxiety. My mother leaves to go back to Louisiana, and I feel very alone and have difficulty bonding with my beautiful baby boy. All of my attention was on my husband and what he was doing. As you can imagine, I could no longer interact or go about my relationship with this woman and my husband as normal, so I confronted them both. I ask her if she was having an affair with my husband, and she denied it. I asked my husband, and he denied it as well. Okay, where do I go from here?

Something in me is telling me to search and seek to reveal the truth. So, I became obsessed with trying to find evidence of this affair with this so-called friend. I am checking his phone, following him every chance I get. I focused on finding evidence of their infidelity, and I used all of my energy in this endeavor. I remember I would cry all the time because I thought, Lord, why me? Why am I going through this storm in my marriage? I thought I had the perfect marriage. I was exhausted, and each day it was difficult for me to process my thoughts. To say it plainly, I was a "hot mess."

One day I was looking at my baby and getting ready to do something related to chasing down my husband, and I heard God say, "you made him your God. He is not your God; I Am." I could not believe what I had heard. I began to think about how I had stopped reading the word of God, stop praying, and sadly had not given my new baby the affection and full nurturing he needed from me. Why? Because I was chasing another god, which was my husband. I had made him my God, and God was not having it! Exodus 20:3 says, "*You shall have no other gods before Me.*" (NKJV)

God desires that He be the only one we worship. Only God can satisfy our longing for love and acceptance. He is the only one who can give us peace and navigate us through this life. If we resolve ourselves to give our mind, body, and soul to another human, they will almost certainly mismanage our life, and we will never come into the truth of who we are. God has not made any provision for us to make each other, or for that matter, anything else, our God. Jehovah is the only true living God, and He desires that we serve Him because serving Him is good for us, and we were created to do so.

God used all of my chasings and checking my husband's phone to reveal the real issue in my heart. He showed me who was sitting on the throne of my heart, and it was not Him. God wanted all of me; He wanted my affection and my attention. I realized that throughout my marriage (at the time we were married six years), I had forgotten about myself and God and had placed all of my focus and energy on ensuring my husband's goals and aspirations were fulfilled. God wanted me to find out what plans and aspirations He had for my life. He did not want me to ignore the seeds He had placed inside of me and focus on cultivating the plans and purposes of my husband. He wanted me to find my purpose in Him.

I was in this storm, and the mental, emotional and physical winds were blowing all around me, but God was speaking, and I was trying my best to listen. I remember crying out to the Lord, with tears rolling down my face, asking him to help me get out of the storm I was experiencing. I did not want to live my life or have a marriage that consisted of chasing my husband down, checking his phone, and monitoring his every move. I wanted to pursue God to the same effort, and if not even more than I was pursuing my husband, but I did not know which way to turn. During this time, all of the people I considered an associate or friend thought I was crazy and wrong for accusing this friend of mine of cheating with my husband, so they quickly distanced themselves from me. But I believe this was also by divine design. God made sure I did not have anyone around me to lean heavenly upon or to turn to for help. He knew I had a tendency to look to man to give me purpose, so I believe He made sure I did not have any opportunities to establish anyone as a god in my life. He began to distance me from those who were familiar with the situation.

However, my hairdresser, whom I had just met, knew the anguish and emotional pain I was going through and supported me. She allowed me to share my heart of what I was going through and encouraged me to focus on my baby and not my husband. She was one of those women who did not hold back in telling you the truth, so she would say to me, "Cynthia, get it together," when I would be tempted to chase down my husband or try to find evidence of his suspected infidelity. Her words did not always make me feel good, but I knew they were pushing me out of the eye of my storm and into my purpose. God used her to encourage me to go to college and find out what God wanted me to do. Some people left me when the waves and wind blew, but God brought her into my life as a lighthouse. Her words of encouragement and tough talk gave me strength in more ways than one, and for that, I am so thankful for her, Ms. Darlene Johnson.

I was still going to church, but not as frequently. The reason being, I was all over the place and could not get it together. But on this one particular Sunday morning, I decided to visit this Baptist Church and not go to the church I had been attending. As I sat in the church listening to the worship, tears began to run down my face. I did not know why I chose this church on this Sunday morning, but I was there. When the co-pastor got up to preach the word, she gave the title of her message, which was "Driving Under the Influence of Satan." As I sat and listened to the sermon, I thought, this is me. For months, Satan has been influencing my behavior. I had allowed him to control my mind and my emotions. He could no longer write his lies in my book, so he created a map for my feelings, and I was following it to a "t." I was under his influence, and he loved every moment of watching me walk in anxiety and fear.

At the end of the sermon, the pastor asked if anyone needed prayer, so I immediately ran up to the altar and cried my eyes out even more. I did not want Satan to be my influencer any longer. Someone prayed with me, and I got sober at that altar. I made up in my heart and mind that I was no longer going to focus on my husband's activities, but I would focus on God's activities and what He was doing in my life. When I got up from that altar, I felt peace. I drove home with a new determination to make God my priority and not my husband. The next few months were very challenging in my marriage because I was focused on God. I had become so entrenched in reading the bible and seeking God's face that it frightened my husband and made him angry.

Ephesians 6:12 says, *"For we wrestle not against flesh and blood, but against principalities, against powers, against the rulers of the darkness of this world, against spiritual wickedness in high places.* (KJV) The principalities and powers that influenced my husband's behavior were upset that I no longer bowed down to the requirements I had followed for years. I had dethroned my husband as my all and my source and placed him in his rightful place. I allowed Jesus to be Lord in my life. Remember,

Satan will use anyone to keep you from reaching your potential and fulfilling your purpose in Christ. I'm not saying you should not honor and respect your spouse. We should honor, respect, and love our spouse, but not at the expense of forgetting about Jesus, our Savior. It is unhealthy for anyone to give their life completely over to someone else and trust them more than they trust God.

So, the question everyone asks me when I share my testimony is, "was it true? Did your husband have an affair with your friend?" And my answer is, "I don't know." I confronted them both, and they both denied the affair. Trying to find the evidence to support what I thought happened was costing me too much. I was drowning in searching, seeking, and investigating. It cost me my peace, my rest, and time with my newborn baby. As much as I tried in my strength to expose the truth of their relationship by chasing my husband and checking his phone, I did not uncover any "smoking gun" evidence.

I looked at my life and knew I did not want to lose my mind in this situation and decided to lay everything at the feet of Jesus. My prayer was, "Lord, if you want to bring light and truth to the situation, then bring it and help me through it. If you choose not to, then give me the wisdom to walk through this storm and come out knowing who you are and who I am in You." I also prayed every day that God would heal the brokenness in my husband and help us process our emotions. Some days I would be okay, while other days, I would be furious and feel the hurt of the idea of infidelity. But the Lord would bring to my remembrance the sermon I heard in church on that Sunday, "Driving Under the Influence of Satan." I remembered the feeling of being under Satan's influence and did not want to go back to that place.

I was intentional about placing everything, my anger, fears, concerns, and tears, at the feet of Jesus and allowed Him to minister to me through His word. The more I read God's word, fasted, and prayed, my faith got stronger. I began to be bold and confident in prayer. I was casting down the images and illusions the enemy would try and use to get me back under His influence. Through God's grace, mercy, and divine insight, I was finally able to see the demonic assignments against my marriage and my life. I was determined not to allow Satan to influence my emotions or my life. He did not have a right to, and I would no longer make it easy for him to do so. My life belonged to Jesus, and I was going to be under His influence!

God balanced my relationship with my husband and gave me divine insight into how a marriage should look. Some strongholds had to be broken, but Jesus helped me day by day and gave me instructions step-by-step to navigate my relationship with my husband.

There were a lot of things God revealed to me, and I learned through my storm. God showed me I had the power and authority to use the spiritual weapons of warfare to fight for my life, marriage, and children. He taught me how to love, honor, and properly respect my husband. He showed me that I had His boldness. When I prayed, fasted, and read His word, this boldness would effectively dismantle everything trying to destroy what God was doing in my life. Psalm 138:3 says, *on the day I called, you answered me; You made me bold with strength in my soul*. (NKJV) Jesus did this for me! I called on Him, and He gave me boldness. And the most important thing I learned through my storm was that I had a purpose. God knew me and had a divine plan for my life. I was not insignificant; I was not inadequate; I was a woman of God called to speak His word. God called me to pray for the masses and help others see their purpose in Christ. When I look back at this time in my life, I can't help but believe God allowed this storm to occur to reveal His purpose and push me into my destiny!

If I had not gone through my storm, I would not be where I am today, writing this book and preparing to write many other books. I would not be speaking and encouraging women from all walks of life to pursue Jesus so they can discover their identity and purpose and live beyond their expectations. I would not have the boldness in prayer to believe God for the impossibilities in my life and the lives of others. Satan may have instigated the storm, but Jesus navigated me through it, and I landed right where I needed to be with everything, He wanted me to have. Yes, I lost some things in the storm, but what I lost was never meant to remain in my life. The feelings of fear, sadness, and inadequacy were all lies from the enemy, and I will never again be a vessel where these lies can flourish.

If you are going through a storm and you are experiencing some of the same things I experienced, I encourage you to lay everything at the feet of Jesus. Don't fasten your heart, mind, and soul to the lies of the enemy. Satan comes to steal, kill and destroy. He wants you to remain under his influence so he can steal your identity, kill your purpose and destroy your legacy! Cast down his lies and all the negative thoughts he is trying to influence you with. 2 Corinthians 10:5 says, *"casting down (vain) imaginations, and every high thing that exalted itself against the knowledge of God, and bringing into captivity every thought to the obedience of Christ."* (NKJV)

God, through Jesus, has given us the power and authority to cast down unfruitful thoughts that do not align with His word. During my storm, I would say this scripture multiple times a day because I was determined not to allow Satan's vain imaginations to rule me and lead me back to a place of fear and anxiety. It was not always easy, but God gave me the strength to keep declaring His word, and it shifted things in my life and my marriage. God wants to make a shift in your life, so let go of what you are holding on to. It is not working, and it is adding stress and anxiety to your life. Hold on to God's hand. He wants to bring you to the other side of your storm with substance and reveal your purpose.

If you have experienced a spouse's unfaithfulness and there is evidence of infidelity, I'm in no way implying all you have to do is cast your cares unto the Lord, and everything will be alright. God has brought my husband and me through a long healing process, and we are still working on areas in our marriage. If you are going through a tough time in your marriage, I encourage you to pray and seek help from a licensed marriage counselor or a Christian counselor. They will be able to walk you and your spouse through the healing process of infidelity. I am sharing how God led me through my experience with infidelity; your process may look different. But what I do know is God can heal and restore your marriage and your heart. Psalm 50:15 says, ***"Call upon Me in the day of trouble; I will deliver you, and you shall glorify Me."*** (NKJV) So, call on Him, and He will answer you, and your life and your marriage will glorify Him!

CHAPTER 7

"FOCUS IS A WEAPON"

As the rains and the wind began to settle in my storm, the Lord began to show me other things in my life that would hinder my growth and potential in Him if I did not address them. One of the things He revealed to me was that I lacked focus. The definition of "focus" is to direct towards a particular point or purpose. Our purpose in Christ will require us to stay focused on each assignment He gives us to fulfill. There are distractions around us attempting to steal our "God opportunities." We are bombarded with the cares of this life, and if we are not careful, months, years and even decades will go by without us even knowing that we have missed pivotal "God opportunities."

Focus has always been a challenge for me. I struggled in school to remain focused, and even now, I have to make sure that I am focused on one thing, or I will get busy with many things that are time wasters. God knows I struggle to remain focused, so He will often remind me through a dream or prophetic word that I need to be intentional about staying focused on what He is calling me to do. In 2006 I attended a conference in Jacksonville, FL. A woman of God prophesied the below over my life- "You can be busy with a lot of things. But if you will remain focused, God is going to reveal dimensions to you- but you are going to have to remain focused."

I will never forget this prophetic word and think about it every time the Lord tells me to complete an assignment. It also reminds me that distraction is my kryptonite, especially when it relates to my Calling. Before the storm, I did not have divine insight into what hindered me from accomplishing my professional, spiritual, and personal goals. I was oblivious to this hindrance and thought I had no control over distractions. I began to see how focus would need to be made a priority in my life. I knew if I wanted to remain effective and committed to living beyond my expectations and fulfilling my purpose in Christ, focus would be one of my main life themes. I needed to spend my time just as I would spend my money-with intentionality, wisdom, and with purpose. Time is just as valuable as our money, and how we spend it and where we spend it matters. Just as we invest our money and expect a return, we should be investing our time with the expectation of a return as well. If you are spending time doing activities and don't see a tangible or spiritual return, you may want to change your spiritual portfolio.

My focus and obedience to the leading of the Holy Spirit were essential during my storm. The pressures of what I was going through forced me to remain focused. I had to listen attentively to the direction of the Holy Spirit every day because Satan's devices were coming at me from different directions.

Romans 8:14 says, "*For as many are led by the Spirit of God, these are the sons of God.*" I knew I had to be led by the Spirit of God, so every big or little decision I had to make, I submitted it to the Lord. Whether it was eating somewhere, connecting with people, or who I should talk with on the phone. You may be thinking, "Cynthia, wasn't this a little overboard?" And my response is, "yes, it may have been." But I realized early on that I did not want to re-do the storm I had just come through, so I focused on doing what God wanted me to do and not what others wanted of me. I decided to fix my mind on Jesus!

The bible tells us that we ought not to be ignorant of the enemy's devices. One of the enemy's devices is the Spirit of "distraction." He has used this one for centuries, yet many of us have fallen prey to it. Have you ever set a time to write, read the bible, spend time with God, and then the phone rings, a friend stops by, or something else comes up? These are what I'll call "distractions on assignment."

I mentioned Ephesians 6:10-12 scripture in a previous chapter. Still, it bears repeating, *"**For we do not wrestle (fight) against flesh and blood, but against principalities, against powers, against rulers of the darkness of this age, against spiritual hosts of wickedness in heavenly places.**"* Our fight is not natural but spiritual. Every distraction we experience in the natural has a spiritual foundation. In other words, if you struggle to complete what God has called you to do, there is likely a battle going on in the Spirit for your time. The good thing is, we don't have to go into these battles alone. God not only shows us the enemy's tactics, but He shows us how to fight. He tells us what weapons to use, and when to engage the enemy. Ephesians 6:10-18 says, "*Finally, be strong in the Lord and his mighty power. Put on the full armor of God so that you can take your stand against the devil's schemes. For our struggle is not against flesh and blood, but against the rulers, against the authorities, against the powers of this dark world and the spiritual forces of evil in the heavenly realms. Therefore, put on the full armor of God so that when the day of evil comes, you may be able to stand your ground, and after you have done everything, to stand. Stand firm then, with the belt of truth buckled around your waist, with the breastplate of righteousness in place, and with your feet fitted with the readiness that comes from the gospel of peace. In addition to all this, take up the shield of faith, with which you can extinguish all the flaming arrows of the evil one. Take the helmet of salvation and the sword of the Spirit, which is the word of God. And pray in the Spirit on all occasions with all kinds of prayers and requests. With this in mind, be alert and always keep on praying for all the saints.*" (NIV)

At each level of Satan's attack, God reveals methods to counter-attack and dismantle his strongholds. When I finally grasp how my focus impacted my progress in pursuing my purpose, I saw my life changed for the better in all areas of my life-personally, mentally, and spiritually. When the strongholds and yokes associated with my storm tried to resurface in my life, I took the word of God (the bible) and focused on what God promised me and not on what I was hearing. I was determined not to go back into the storm, so I focused on God and who He was.

Even though I was focused, Satan was also focused on getting me back under his influence. One morning I woke up and could not settle my thoughts. I felt my mind going back to old ways of thinking and anxiety rising in my heart and body. Satan was overly aggressive that day and wanted my attention. I was having a hard time reading my word, praying, and even thinking the right thoughts. The old feeling of anxiety and worry was trying to creep into my heart and was tempting me to declare things out of my mouth that would have led me back into the storm. All of a sudden, I said, "Okay, Satan, every time you tell me I won't make it out of this, or my situation won't change, I am going to focus on praising and worshipping God." Jeremiah 17:14 says, *"Heal me, O Lord, and I shall be healed; Save me, and I shall be saved, For You*

Are My Praise. So, I got a song and prayer in my mouth and began to declare them simultaneously. Within a few minutes, my thoughts shifted to the goodness of Jesus, and I no longer heard the voice of Satan. He had fled because he could not endure hearing my voice praise God. I focused on what I was created to do, worship God, and found relief from Satan's attack. Not only did I get relief from Satan's attacks at that moment, but I discovered that praise, worship, and prayer are spiritual weapons of warfare. In the heat of the battle, my focus was on praying, praising, and worshiping God, and it put Satan to flight. Satan had no room to influence my thoughts when I opened my mouth and declared the beautiful attributes of God and His son Jesus.

If Satan is trying to lead you away from focusing on Jesus and tempting you to return to the winds and rain of your storm, use the spiritual weapons of praise, worship, and prayer. You cannot go back into that storm. Tell Satan you are focused only on where God is taking you, not to the places he wanted you to remain. Be intentional with your focus. Keep your focus on Jesus' plans and not Satan's plots and schemes. When we focus on God and His ways, it becomes a weapon used against Satan. Satan does not like focused Believers in Jesus

Christ. When we are focused, we will give birth to and complete every assignment God has ordained us to achieve. Every time you focus on Jesus, you defeat Satan.

CHAPTER 8

"I AM AN OVERCOMER"

God gave me the strength to get to the other side of my storm, and I finally realized who I was, which was a woman of purpose and an "Overcomer." While going through the storm, I did not see myself as an "Overcomer." I saw myself as defeated with no purpose. But it was my storm that revealed my "Overcomer" attributes.

God had already called me an "Overcomer," even while I was in my mother's womb. I am no medical professional, but let me try to explain it in medical terms. On or about day 14 in the menstrual cycle, a sudden surge in luteinizing hormone causes the ovary to release an egg. The released egg begins its five-day travel through a narrow and hollow structure called the fallopian tube headed to the uterus. Out of the 300,000 eggs in my mother's womb, for some reason, God chose me to be released that month. And despite the narrow and hallow conditions I had to go through during my journey to life, God kept me moving in the direction of fertilization by the sperm. My mother and father connected in intimacy, and my life began to form in my mother's womb. Jeremiah 1:5 says, "Before I formed you in the womb, I knew you; before you were born, I sanctified you...

God knew who I was before I had life in my mother's womb and even on this earth. He formed me and knew who I would be before I was in my mother's womb. He pushed me to life in my mother's womb, and He continues to push me to life now that I am outside her womb. If you've made it through the narrow and hollow places of the reproductive system, you can make it through the narrow and hollow places of this life because you are an "Overcomer!

We were on God's mind before we were even born, and we are still on His mind now. He is not going to desert us, but He will lead us to life. He has a Spiritual Global Positioning System (GPS) in our hearts and has never lost track of our life. Even when I thought He was nowhere to be found and had left me alone to deal with life's struggles, He was continuously tracking me. Even when I was walking through fear, inadequacy, and sadness and could not shake these feelings, He was tracking me. Even when I ignored His voice to live for Him and fell in love with sin, He was tracking me. Even when I thought I would lose my mind in my storm, He was tracking me. When I was tracking the winds and waves of my storms, He had His eyes on me.

He wasn't going to let me drown, fall apart, or go under. There were times I thought, "this is it; I'm not going to make it." Then all of a sudden, I would remember a scripture my mother had read to me or a song we sang in the choir growing up; I would say the scripture or sing the song, and I would find myself treading the waters and not drowning under the waves and winds of my storm.

When I think about the things I experienced in my life, the ups and downs, I take a deep breath-inhaling and exhaling. My breathing reminds me that as long as I have breath in my body and keep Jesus as the center of my life, I will get through the storms of life and overcome every obstacle before me. It was never God's plan for me to be stripped of my title as an "Overcomer" because of my mistakes. Furthermore, He did not give Satan the authority to rob me of this title while going through my storm. I am an "Overcomer', and I declare that you are an "Overcomer" also.

1 John 5:4 says, *"for whatever is born of God overcomes the world. And this is the victory that has overcome the world—our faith.* (NKJV) We are all born of God, so when we walk in faith in Jesus Christ, we can overcome anything that stands in the way of our purpose. The storms in your life want you to relinquish your title as an "Overcomer," but guess what, you and I get to tell the storm, "Not today, Jesus is tracking me, and He will not allow me to go under because I am an Overcomer!"

Overcomer is who God says you are, so believe Him!

CHAPTER 9

"PURPOSE WAS ALWAYS IN THE STORM"

In the early 1990s, Yolanda Adams released a gospel song titled "Through the Storm." I love to hear the live recording of this song by Ms. Adams. The way she sings this song gives me chills. If you have not heard her sing this song live, I encourage you to find it on YouTube and listen to it; the music will bless you. All the lyrics to this song are a blessing, but I want to share my favorite ones with you below:

While riding through the storm
Jesus holds me in His arms
I am not afraid
Of the stormy winds and the waves

Though the tides become high
He holds me while I ride
I found safety in His arms
While riding through the storm

I have no fear of the raging seas
Knowing Jesus is there with me
He can speak to the wind and the waves
And make them behave

When I was going through my storm, I listened to this song, and it gave me much comfort. Even when the seas are raging in our storms, we find safety in the arms of Jesus. We also get the opportunity to trust Jesus more than we ever would have and see Him for who He is, which is Our Lord and Savior. It is not fun, nor is it comfortable when we are in the midst of the storm. Our life changes and everything familiar becomes unfamiliar. I thought I had a perfect life and was very content. But God wanted me to see who I was in Him and not the person I had created-fashioned by hurt, pain, disappointment, and lies of the enemy. He wanted me to see my true authentic self, the woman of God He created in His image to do His good works.

I experienced heartache, pain, disappointment and cried many tears during my storm, but all these things served God's purpose for my life. I learned through my storm that my purpose is to help other women "Live Beyond their Expectations, by compelling them through the word of God (the bible) to surrender fully to Jesus so He can show them who they are in Him. I learned through my storm that God has called me to encourage women through prayer and mentorship to pursue and walk out their God assignments so that He can be glorified in their life and add increase and value to everything they touch.

I hid in the shadows for a long time. I was afraid to step out and do what God called me to do because I did not believe God could use someone like me; I was so wrong. And if you are reading this book and believe God cannot use you, I want to tell you that you are So Wrong as well! Not only can God use you, but He wants to use you; He delights in using you. He wants to use you to reach women and men of all races and nationalities. You may be in the process of going through a storm, but I want to declare over your life that you are coming out with substance and God's purpose for your life.

Through my storm, God showed me I was bold and confident. I did not have to walk with my head down, content with what life was offering me. There was more for me in Jesus, and I had every right to go after and apprehend everything He had for me with no apologies! My purpose to coach and mentor women to leave fear, inadequacy, and sadness behind and step out in faith was always a part of the storm. I needed to know who I was before I can help someone else discover who they are. As women, we must gain His insight and accept the truth that we have gifts and talents that need to be shared with others- not for our glory but God's glory. We cannot leave this earth with seed still in our spiritual womb. We have to give birth, and sometimes we will give birth in the storm.

God called Esther for such a time as this. She was positioned with a purpose to save a nation. You and I have also been positioned with purpose. We are all women called for such a time as this. It may be in a different city, region, or country, but God wants to use us to tell the world who He is, and He wants to demonstrate His power through our lives to make a difference in the lives of others.

Everything I went through catapulted me into my purpose. It was the storm that revealed God's unfailing love for me and exposed the hatred and lies of Satan. I am confident in who the Lord is and His faithfulness towards seeing me do all He called me to do. I trust the Lord, and I am committed to following His way for the rest of my life. Before 1999, I could not have uttered these words because I thought I could never measure up or do anything significate for God.

Now I know without any reservation or hesitation that Jesus loves me and wants to display His word through my life. He is the one who gives me the strength to hold on to Him through the storms of life. He gives me the supernatural ability to remain focused on Him, even when the winds are blowing and the seas are raging. I will hold on to Jesus through the storms of life. I am fully persuaded that God's purpose for our life will always prevail when our hearts, mind, and eyes are fixed upon Jesus as we go through the storms of life.

CONCLUSION

It's no coincidence you have read this entire book. As you conclude my book, I pray you have gotten the revelation knowledge of how much God loves you and wants you to know your life has meaning. The storms of life will try to dictate your destiny and lead you to believe God is not with you, but this is far from the truth; He is with you. Don't give in to the pressures of your storm or Satan lies. Allow God to dismantle every lie with the truth of His word. You are predestined to walk in your purpose. Romans 8:30 says, *"**Whom he predestined, these He also called; whom He called, these He also justified; and whom He justified, these He also glorified.**"* (NKJV)

I encourage you to change your perspective. Look at Jesus and not the storm. If you look at the storm, you will sink under the pressure of the wind just like Peter did in Matthew chapter 14. Peter began to sink because He took his eyes off of Jesus. God is an awesome and loving God. He did not leave us on this earth to fend for ourselves. He sent us His son to help us get to the other side of our storms so we can know our purpose is in Him.

Please remember, we don't come out of our storms empty-handed. When we focus on Jesus and not the storm, we come out full of substance and with divine resources ready to be released for the Glory of God. During my storm, I discovered who Jesus was and how much He wanted me to live a life dedicated to Him and His plans for my life; I found my purpose. I'm no different than anyone else. God desires that you find your purpose, even in the storms of life. God can lead you back to where you need to be in Him; trust Him.

Get on your knees and ask Him to lead you right into your purpose during your storm. I know the winds are blowing, and people are saying you won't make it, but I tell you that you can and will make it to the other side of this storm, and great will be your testimony and reward. Please don't keep quiet, and don't be ashamed of what you have gone through; share your story. Tell everyone you can of the goodness of God in your life. Revelation

12:11 says, ***and they overcame him by the blood of the Lamb and the word of their testimony, and they loved not their lives unto the death***. (KJV)

The blood of Jesus Christ is powerful, and when we couple it with our testimony of who He is in our lives, the enemy is defeated. Don't be ashamed to share with others your testimony of the breakthrough and deliverance you experienced and the purpose you discovered during your storm.

I am confident and fully persuaded that God will reveal his purpose in your life when you fix your eyes on Jesus during the storms!

Cynthia B. Jackson
Founder- Speaking Encouraging Words-S.E.W.
"Live Beyond Your Expectation"

References/Sources:

Source: Musixmatch
Songwriters: Kirk Franklin
Something About the Name Jesus lyrics © Bridge Building Music, Kerrion Publishing, Lilly Mack Music

Source: Musixmatch
Songwriters: Varn Mckay
Through the Storm lyrics © Schaff Music Publishing

https://my.clevelandclinic.org/health/articles/11585-pregnancy-ovulation-conception--getting-pregnant

New King James Version (NKJV)
King James Version (KJV)
New International Version (NIV)

Revision from book Titled- "Contending for Your Destiny – Finding Your Purpose through Life Trials.

Cynthia B. Jackson

"Finding Purpose in the Storm" is the manifestation of God's word for my life. This book is my testimony of how Jesus revealed Himself to me when the storms of life were trying to take me under to take me out. Through my storm, God showed me who I was and what I was I was capable of doing for Him and through Him. When life winds and seas calmed down around me, I finally saw who Christ wanted me to be- I found my Purpose!

My prayer is as you read my story, you will find encouragement not to give up or give in to the storms of life that are attempting to capsize your Purpose in Christ. God has a divine word that must be fulfilled in your life! As you read each chapter, I believe you will begin to see yourself living beyond life storms and fulfilling what God has called you to do!

Cynthia B. Jackson is the founder of Speaking Encouraging Words-S.E.W. S.E.W. focuses on "SEWing" God's word in our hearts, so His word can be lived out in our lives. She is an author, transformational speaker, teacher, and prophetic intercessor. Her passion is encouraging, edifying, and mentoring others to solidify their Purpose and Identity in Jesus Christ. Through words of encouragement and prophetic insight, she has witness lives transformed and generational curses dismantled, bringing deliverance and wholeness to the lives of many.

Cynthia serves as the President of the Board of Directors for Women of Purpose, a non-profit organization created to see women Discover, Develop and Activate their God-given Purpose. She also serves as a prophetic and ministry leader in the body of Christ. She has a Bachelor of Science Degree in Human Resources Management and over 20 years of experience in Human Resources Management/Workforce Planning in the Federal Government.

She is passionate about speaking life and believes when we speak life, we will "Live Beyond our Expectations!

CONTACT THE AUTHOR

Cynthia B. Jackson
info@cynthiabjackson.com
www.cynthiabjackson.com

Made in the USA
Middletown, DE
28 September 2022